Magnetic Magic

by Terry Catasús Jennings

illustrated by Andrea Gabriel

Dena held the board carefully with one hand. On top, a paper clip moved. The little kids at the pool watched, mouths wide open, eyes fixed on the paper clip.

"It's magic," Dena said.

Except it wasn't. It was magnetism.

She had worked on the trick for weeks. She learned to move a magnet under the board without moving her arm. She learned to talk like a magician, making the little kids think of the paper clip and not of her hand below. She practiced until she could do the trick perfectly.

She could also make two magnets pull together, or push apart, but she didn't have to practice. That's what magnets do naturally. They attract and repel. Dena could make one magnet hover over another. If she stacked several magnets just right, she could turn the pile upside down and the magnets would still stick.

She floated a lodestone on a thin piece of wood, spun the board, and predicted where the stone would point when it stopped. The little kids squealed when she "guessed" right. Older kids became interested in her magic, too.

But loadstones aren't magic either. They are magnets. They'll always end up pointing north.

When she made a magnet look
like it was floating down a
thick pipe, everyone went wild.

One day, a new boy named Enrique came to the pool. He was visiting his grandfather for the summer.

"That's not magic," Enrique said. "It's magnetism."

"Shh!" Dena whispered. "Don't tell on me. The kids love it."

"You shouldn't fool them," Enrique said.

"The big kids know . . . "

"But you're fooling the little ones."

Dena knew fooling the little kids wasn't nice, but she loved doing it! She kept on performing.

The next day, Enrique handed her a map. "I bet you can't find this place," he dared. The date on Enrique's map was 1905.

A note said, "Start at the front door of the elementary school. Walk 1000 feet northwest to find a surprise in the hole at the bottom of the oak tree."

Dena loved treasure maps. Using compasses was the best part of magnetism. She ran home to get a map of her town, her compass, and a parallel ruler.

She spread out her town map. She placed one straight edge of the ruler on the compass rose to find northwest (315°). Then she slid the other straight edge so that one end touched the location of old elementary school's door. She used the map's scale to plot a position about 1000 feet from the door. Her plotting told her to look between the restrooms and the adult softball field at the community park.

Dena estimated that it would take 800 of her steps to walk 1000 feet.

Dena started at the door of the school. Using her compass, she and her friends walked on a bearing of 315°.

When they arrived at the area
where the oak tree should be,
they didn't find it or the treasure.

"Something's wrong," Dena said.

"Maybe the tree died," Enrique said.
He could barely keep from laughing.

Dena was so angry she was sure smoke was coming out of her ears. Was Enrique trying to fool her?

Dena re-checked her work when she got home. Why couldn't she find the tree? Maybe Enrique was right. The tree had died and that's why he was laughing. The madder she got, the more her brain worked. Thinking, thinking. She had to find that tree . . . or its stump.

"I've got it," Dena shouted even though no one was around to hear her. She pictured a tall stump with a triangular hole on the bottom. It was behind the outfield fence at the little league field. She saw it every time she played center field. Maybe that was the tree on the old map.

She ran to the little league field. She was right! A metal box lay inside the hole in the stump.

It was a long way from where she walked the first time. When she plotted the new place on her map, the compass direction was six degrees off.

The next day, Dena took Enrique and the older kids to the stump at the little league field. Like a magician performing a trick, she opened the box. A note inside promised a sundae at Mr. Scoops' Ice Cream Shop for anyone who found it.

"You tricked me," Dena said on the way to the ice cream shop.

"Not me," Enrique said. "The map was right in 1905. Earth's magnetic field moves. Magnetic north is in a different place now."

"You shouldn't have fooled me," she said.

"Why not?" Enrique shot back. "You fool the little kids all the time."

At Mr. Scoops', Enrique's grandfather,
the owner, treated everyone to sundaes.
He told them he used the map to show
Enrique how Earth's magnetic field moves.

Dena was glad to have the ice cream, but she sure wasn't happy she'd been fooled.

The next day, Dena did her show at the pool again.

"I like your magic," one of the little kids said.

"It's not magic," Dena said. "It's magnetism." She showed him how it worked. No more fooling.

For Creative Minds

Magnets

Magnetism is a force. The ancient people in the town of Magnesia in Asia Minor—now Turkey—found that some stones attracted and repelled each other. They also attracted things made of iron. They called these stones "magnets." We now call them "lodestones." They are likely formed when a piece of iron ore is struck by lightning. The lightning aligns all the iron particles in the same direction, creating poles. These rocks attract and repel, a force we call magnetism.

So what is a magnet? A magnet is a piece of iron in which all the atoms point in the same direction. All north-seeking atoms point one way (North-seeking pole or N) and all the south-seeking atoms point in the opposite direction (South-seeking pole or S). Electricity, like lightning, can make magnets. Now we make magnets by passing a piece of iron through an electric field. The electric field aligns all the iron atoms in the same direction. The N poles of magnets pull toward—attract—the S poles of other magnets. The N poles of magnets push away—repel—the N poles of other magnets. The S poles of magnets also repel the S poles of other magnets. An easy way to think of this is to say that like poles repel and unlike (or opposite) poles attract.

Earth itself is like a giant magnet, with a north pole and a south pole. Around the year 1000, the Chinese discovered that a steel needle rubbed against a lodestone and allowed to swing freely would always point toward the north. Steel is made mostly of iron. The Chinese began using these needles as compasses.

Earth has a magnetic field around it. The funny thing is, as Dena found out, the north magnetic pole is not the same as the north geographic pole. The north and south magnetic poles move. The purple line on this map shows the change in magnetic north from 1905 to 2016.

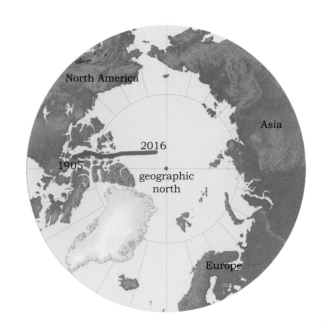

Map Skills

To find your way from one place to another, you need to know at least two things: the direction you should travel and the distance you need to go.

A compass is a tool that uses a magnet to determine direction. Directions on a compass are measured in degrees (°), with 360° in a circle. North is 000°, or 360°. If you face north, east (090°) is the direction to your right, south (180°) is behind you, and west (270°) is to your left.

The needle of a compass always points to magnetic north. When you use a compass, hold it flat and rotate the compass so that the number 000° lines up under the needle. Then you can walk in the direction you need to go, keeping 000° lined up under the needle the whole time.

Maps have a compass rose to show which direction on the map is north. Dena used the compass rose on the map to find the direction from the school to the treasure. She used her compass to make sure she was going the right way.

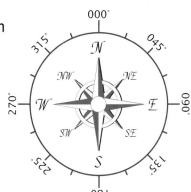

But even if you know what direction to go, you can still travel too far or not far enough and miss your destination completely. When you travel from one place to another, you need to know both the direction and the distance.

Maps have scales that show how the distance on the map relates to distance in real life. For a map of a town, one inch on the map might represent one mile. For a map of the whole world, one inch on the map could equal 100 or 1000 miles. Dena used the scale to know how far she should walk.

Magnetic north shifts over time. The treasure map Dena used was from 1905, when magnetic north was in a different place. When she plotted the treasure's location on the modern map of her town, her direction was a few degrees off. Even though she walked the right distance, she couldn't find the treasure because she had gone the wrong direction.

Make Magnetic Magic

Move Paperclips

For this trick you will need:

- metal paper clips
- magnets
- stiff cardboard, like a game board
- cloth covering (optional)

Hold the board with one hand or put it on a stand. Place the paper clips on top of the cardboard. Make the paper clips move by moving the magnet underneath. Be careful you only move your hand, not your arm; bend at the wrist.

You can make this trick more like a magic show by covering your cardboard with a piece of cloth. Remember, part of the show is talking to your audience so they forget about the hand under the cardboard. Magic!

Float a Lodestone

For this trick you'll need:

- lodestone
- string
- marker

Before you perform this trick, use a compass to figure out where north is and which end of the stone points north. Mark that end with a marker. Predict which way the stone will point when it stops (that would be north on the compass). Float the loadstone on a piece of wood in a tub, or hang it from a string. Give the stone a twirl. Magic!

Make a Magnet Hover

For this trick you will need:

· two or more circular magnets with holes in the middle.
· pencil or a dowel

Put the magnets on the pencil or dowel so that they repel each other. If the magnets attract each other and snap together, take one off and flip it around. Hold the pencil pointing up, with your fingers at its base. Watch the top magnet hover. Magic!

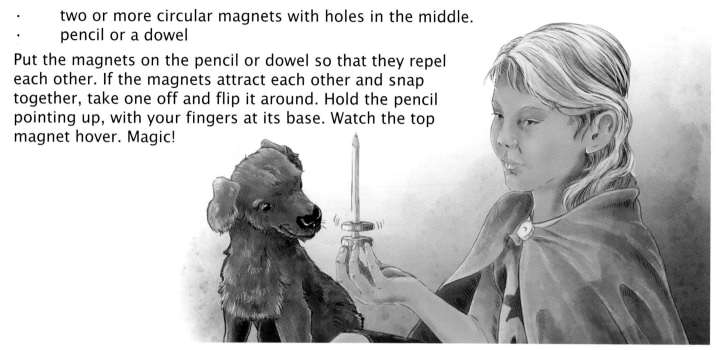

Float a Magnet in a Pipe

For this trick you'll need:

· copper or aluminum pipe .75 inches in diameter (from your local hardware store)
· three neodymium disk magnets (.7 inches or less in diameter)
· pebble or other heavy, non-metallic object.

Touch the magnets to the outside of the pipe. Any attraction? Hold the pipe in your hand and drop the heavy, non-metallic object through its center. What happens?

Now hold the pile of magnets above the pipe. Drop them through the pipe's center. What happens now? Turn the magnets over. Is there a difference?

The non-metallic object will drop very quickly, but the magnets will seem to float down the tube. Even though the pipe is not magnetic, the magnets create an electric current which slows their fall. Magic!

To Lou, Teddi, Judy and Kim, who help birth every manuscript.—TCJ

Thanks to William Stone with NOAA's National Geodetic Survey for verifying the accuracy of the magnetism information in this book, and to Lee German, Commander, US Navy-Retired, for verifying the accuracy of the navigation information.

Library of Congress Cataloging in Publication Control Number: 2016019116

9781628558616   English hardcover ISBN
9781628558623   English paperback ISBN
9781628558630   Spanish paperback ISBN
9781628558647   English eBook downloadable ISBN
9781628558654   Spanish eBook downloadable ISBN
Interactive, read-aloud eBook featuring selectable English (9781628558661) and Spanish (9781628558678) text and audio (web and iPad/tablet based) ISBN

Translated into Spanish: *Magia con imanes*

Lexile® Level: AD 560L

Keywords: change over time, character, magnets, magnetism, map, tools and technology (compass), map skills, cardinal directions

Bibliography:
Breslyn, Wayne. "All about Magnets." All about Magnets. University of Maryland, TerpConnect. Web. 21 Aug. 2014.
"Geomagnetism Frequently Asked Questions." National Centers for Environmental Information. NOAA. Web. 21 Aug. 2014.
Goulet, Chris M. "Magnetic Declination." Magnetic Declination FAQ. Rescue Dynamics, 26 Apr. 2014. Web. 21 Aug. 2014.
Kurtus, Ron. "Magnets." School for Champions. Web. 21 Aug. 2014.
Stern, David. "Teaching About Magnetism." The Great Magnet, the Earth. Web. 21 Aug. 2014.

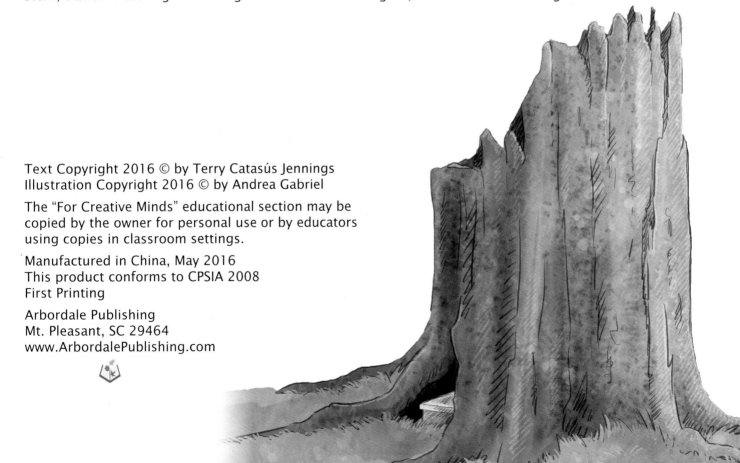

Manufactured in China, May 2016
This product conforms to CPSIA 2008
First Printing

Arbordale Publishing
Mt. Pleasant, SC 29464
www.ArbordalePublishing.com